THE
CROQUET
PLAYER

H. G. WELLS

THE

CROQUET
PLAYER

New York

THE VIKING PRESS

1937

The illustrations are by
CLIFTON LINE

The Croquet Player

Copyright 1937 by H. G. Wells

Printed in U. S. A. by the Haddon Craftsmen

Distributed in Canada by the Macmillan Company of
Canada, Ltd.

CONTENTS

THE
CROQUET
PLAYER

The Croquet Player Introduces Himself

I have been talking to two very queer individuals and they have produced a peculiar disturbance of my mind. It is hardly an exaggeration to say that they have infected me and distressed me with some very strange and unpleasant ideas. I want to set down what it is they have said to me in the first place for my own sake, so as to clear up my thoughts about it. What they told me was fantastic and unreasonable but I shall feel surer about that if I set it down in writing. Moreover I want to get my story into a shape that will enable one or two sympathetic readers to reassure me about the purely imaginative quality of what these two men had to say.

It is a sort of ghost story they unfolded. But it is not an ordinary ghost story. It is much more realistic and haunting and disturbing than any ordinary ghost story. It is not a story of a haunted house or a haunted churchyard or anything so limited. The ghost they told me about was something much larger than that, a haunting of a whole countryside, something that began as an uneasiness and grew into a fear and became by slow degrees a spreading presence. And still it grew—in size, in power and intensity. Until it became a continual overshadowing dread. I do not like this ghost that grows and spreads, even though it does so only in the mind. But I had better begin at the beginning and tell about this story as far as I can, and the manner in which it came to me.

But first I had better give a few particulars about myself. Of course I would rather I did not, but I doubt if you will realize my position without it. I am probably one of the best croquet players alive, and that I am not a bit ashamed of saying. I am also a first-rate archer. One is neither of these things without a considerable amount of discipline and balance in one's make-up. Many people, I know, find me a trifle effeminate and ridiculous because I make croquet my game; they say as much behind my back and at times they betray it to my face, and I admit there have been moments when I have been inclined to agree with them. But on the other hand quite a lot of people seem to like me, everybody calls me Georgie in an affectionate manner, and on the whole I am inclined to like myself. It takes all sorts to make a world and I see no sense in pretending to be the human norm when one is not. Regarded from a certain angle I am no doubt a soft, but all the same I can keep my head and temper at croquet and make a wooden ball perform like a trained animal. Even at tennis I can make some of the fiercer sort extremely cross and silly. And I can do sleight-of-hand tricks, for which you certainly need nerve and complete self-possession, as well as most professionals.

As a matter of fact a lot of these tremendous sporting people, record-breakers, gamblers, and so on, are much more akin to me than they like to think. There is a lot of sham in their pretension to hairiness and virility. At heart they are as tame as I am. They have chosen to be boxed up in games. I suppose cricket and hockey and so on are more gladiatorial than my sort of sport, aviation and motoring more lethal, and gambling more vexatious, but I do not see there is any greater reality in what they do than in what I do. Risk is not reality. They are players just as I am a player. They are enclosed with me in the same pleasant round of harmless and fruitless activities.

I admit I have had an exceptionally uneventful life. I missed the experience of the Great War by a couple of years and my life has always been an extremely sheltered and comfortable one. I was brought up by my paternal aunt, Miss Frobisher, *the* Miss Frobisher of the Barton Chapel Case and the Woman's World Humanity Movement, and it is only slowly that I have come to realize that my upbringing was—if I may be paradoxical—unusually banal. I have led a life largely of negatives and avoidances. I have been trained to keep calm and civil and not react excitedly to surprises. And above all to regard only ordinary decent everyday things seriously.

My aunt took me over at the age of three when my parents divorced and since then she has never let go of me. She is a woman with what, to be frank, one might call a natural hostility to sexual facts, and my parents' misbehaviour—those were the days when the papers published full reports of divorce cases—and some of the details of the affair shocked her extremely. When I went to school at Harton, she took a house close by and entered me as a day-boy, and she did practically the same thing while I was at Keeble. Possibly I am naturally just a little inclined to be what the Americans call a sissy, and this tendency has been favoured by these circumstances.

I have soft hands and an ineffective will. I prefer not to make important decisions. My aunt has trained me to be her constant associate and, with displays and declarations on all possible occasions of an immense maternal passion for me, she has—I know it clearly—made me self-indulgent and dependent. Yet I do not blame her very much or resent it very much. It is how we two have been made. She has always been rich and free to do as she liked, not only with herself but with others, and I have always felt well off and secure. Our lives have been easy so far. Like most well-born, well-off people, we have taken inferiors for granted, servants for granted, and the general good behaviour of the world towards us.

I suppose there are still hundreds of thousands of people in the world as sure of all the material best of life as we are and taking it in the same matter-of-course fashion.

"What shall we do?" we ask. "Where shall we go?" Nobody compels us. We are the floating cream of humanity.

We have a house in Upper Beamish Street, a modest little place in Hampshire, and we move about a lot. My aunt, as many people know, is a very temperamental woman—I do not mean temperamental in any unpleasant sense—and sometimes we are as keen as mustard on this Woman's World Humanity Movement—though I have never clearly understood what it is all about—travelling over the world for it—so far, that is, as there are bathrooms *en suite*, upon which my aunt insists—"making contacts," usually until there is a difficulty over the committee election or something of that sort and my aunt gets disgusted, and then for a year or so we drop Woman's World Humanity and go round wiping up the lawns with croquet champions or winning tassels with our archery. We are both quite extraordinarily good at the long-bow, and my aunt has been painted as Diana by Wilmerdings. But croquet is our especial gift. If we did not shrink from the publicity and vulgarity of it we could certainly be champions. We also play a pretty decent tennis game and our golf might easily be worse, but the popular criticism of tennis has been carried to such high levels that we do not care to be seen playing, and golf we find mixes us up with all sorts of people. Sometimes we just recuperate. Lately we have been recuperating at Les Noupets after a rather discouraging conference of the Woman's World Humanity Movement at Chicago. (The less said about those American delegates the better, but my aunt was fully equal to them.)

That I think is a quite sufficient explanation of myself and my atmosphere. The two club lawns at Les Noupets were excellent, and we found an admirable secretary typist who dealt with my aunt's very extensive correspondence about the movement and particularly with her libel case against Mrs. Glyco-Harriman, taking it all down in shorthand, typing it in the afternoon, and bringing it for revision after tea. There were one or two sets of niceish people with whom a little light conversation was possible without entanglement. Croquet an hour before lunch and perhaps in the afternoon again and dinner at eight. We never play bridge until after dinner; it is our inflexible rule. So that I had a certain amount of time upon my hands while she wrote what would be in the case of anyone without her provocation extremely abusive as well as sarcastic letters, which I devoted chiefly to a morning's walk up the hill to the Perona springs, where I took the waters, rather for fun than with any idea of a cure, and then sat in a state of wholesome idleness on the terrace of the Source Hotel removing the inky taste by appropriately chosen refreshment. My aunt is inclined to a non-alcoholic attitude, but of late years I have found the unobtrusive exercise of my private judgment in such matters not only permissible but better for both of us. I mean I am a more cheerful companion.

I think all that gets me fairly well and now with your permission I will put myself into the background, so to speak—or "frame" perhaps is better—and tell you about the first of these two queer men I met on the Perona terrace.

The
Haunting Fear in
Cainsmarsh

It was while I was sitting out on the terrace in the sun, nibbling a brioche and consuming a harmless vermouth and seltzer, that I first set eyes on Dr. Finchatton. He was two tables away and he was having an almost violent quarrel with a number of books he had got from the Les Noupets tea shop and lending library. He was opening them one after another, reading a few pages, turning them over, muttering, and banging them down on the ground with an emphasis that would have distressed the library people extremely. He looked up and caught my reproving eye. He stared and then smiled.

"Scores of books," he said; "hundreds of books

—and not one worth reading! They're all—*off* it."

There was something comical and irrational about his disgust that amused me. "Then why read them?" I asked. "Reading crowds the memory and prevents one thinking."

"Exactly what I want to do. I came over here to stop thinking—and forget. And I can't." His voice, which to begin with was clear and distinct, rose to an angry note. "Some of these books bore —some irritate. Some even remind me of just what I am trying to forget."

Stepping over his heap of condemned volumes he came, glass and carafe in hand, and without any invitation from me sat down at the table beside me. He looked me in the face with an expression that was at once friendly and slightly quizzical. I know my face is—well, "cherubic"— for a man of thirty-three and it was very evident he appreciated the fact. "Do *you* do much thinking?" he asked.

"A fair amount. I solve the *Times* Crossword Puzzle nearly every day. I play a lot of chess— by correspondence chiefly. And I'm not so bad at bridge."

"I mean real thinking. About things that pursue and worry you and cannot be explained."

"I don't let things worry me," I said.

"Do you happen to be interested in ghosts—and hauntings?"

"I'm neutral. I don't believe in ghosts but I don't *dis*believe in them. If you follow me. I've never seen a ghost. I think there is a lot to be said for spiritualism, quite a lot, in spite of much imposture. I suppose immortality has been proved now by that sort of thing, and that is all to the good. My aunt Miss Frobisher is quite of that opinion. But I feel that the necessary table-rapping and cabinet séances and all that is a job for a specialist."

"But suppose you found there were ghosts all about you?"

"I never have."

"And there's nothing—here for instance—that makes you feel uneasy?"

"Where?" I asked.

"*There*," he said and waved a hand at the tranquil sea and the innocent sky.

"Why should there be?"

"But *is* there?"

"No."

"I envy your insensitiveness—or your imperturbability." He emptied his glass and ordered another half-litre of wine. Either out of ignorance or preference he was drinking red *ordinaire*. "*You* don't feel there is anything? No danger?"

"I never saw a more tranquillizing view. Not a cloud."

"It isn't so with me. . . . I've had some very disturbing experiences. I'm still disturbed. Curious! You feel nothing. Maybe it's just the aftermath of what has happened."

"What *has* happened? And what is the aftermath?"

"I'd like to tell you," he said. "It's rather a yarn, you know."

"Go ahead," said I.

And with that much introduction he began to tell me his story. He was rather disconnected at first and then he settled down to it. He told it to me not as though he particularly wished to tell it to me, but as though he wanted very badly to tell it to someone and hear how it sounded. After he had got started, I interrupted very little.

It was indiscreet of me perhaps to let him begin upon me. I knew nothing of him. I had to ask him for his name before he named himself. Evidently he was queer in some way—I should have remembered that the big house above the town was supposed to be a "Home" for mental cases, a psychotherapeutic institution as they call them nowadays, and the discreet thing for me would have been to have sheered off there and then upon some excuse before his story began.

Yet there was nothing about him to warn me off him. There was nothing eccentric in his manner or indeed in his general appearance. He had the jaded look of a man who doesn't sleep well, a little dark under the eyes, but apart from that he seemed quite all right. He was quietly dressed in the Englishman's usual grey; he wore a coloured shirt and an unobtrusive tie. It was a little askew but that was nothing. Plenty of men never put on their ties straight—though how they can stand it I can't think. It is so easy to get a tie straight. He was decidedly lean and fairly good-looking, with what I suppose one would call a sensitive mouth below his short moustache. He leant forward most of the time with his arms folded under his chest much as a cat folds up its paws. He talked perhaps just a little on the emphatic side but he seemed on the watch to control himself. And as I had a full hour or more to dispose of, before I went down to Les Noupets again, I let him run on, without any attempt to interrupt him or cut him short.

"At first," he said, "I thought it was the marshes."

"What marshes?"

"Cainsmarsh. You have heard of Cainsmarsh?"

I used to be pretty good at geography at school but I could not recall that name. But I did not like to admit my ignorance on the spur of the moment. Something about the word seemed familiar. "Marsh" seemed a clue. Vague suggestions of fenny country, watery expanses, a louring sky, dank black thatch, moored old barges, and the hum of mosquitoes floated across my mind.

"A great district for malaria and rheumatic complaints," he said, confirming my impression. "I bought a practice there. . . . Forgive a touch of autobiography. I did so partly because it was an exceptionally cheap practice and I had to earn a living somehow with my small resources and partly because I wanted to leave the hospital and

London—and rest my brain. I went there jaded and disappointed. It seemed likely to be an easy-going job. There is practically no competition in the marshes, not until you get towards the part they call the Island, where the market-town doctors come out in their cars. The parishes up towards the hills, such as they are, and out towards the saltings are quite beyond their range except for special consultations. I had to go into practice with a minor qualification because of the need I was under for tranquillizing surroundings. . . . I threw up the prospect of a medical degree."

He paused as though he found a difficulty.

"Were you ill?" I inquired, to help him out. "Why *did* you leave the hospital with a minor qualification? Forgive me making a personal remark but you don't look the sort of man who muffs exams."

"I didn't muff exams. In fact I was more than usually ambitious. I worked, I think, too hard. And I was active mentally in other directions. I was keener on politics than most medical students. And I got very keen on social justice and the prevention of war. Very keen on the war question. I had been working on gas. Perhaps I *did* too

much. Perhaps I thought and felt too much. . . .
Yes. . . . Yes, certainly I felt too much. A time
came when the morning paper could upset me
so as to spoil my work for the day.

"From the very beginning of my medical edu-
cation you must know I found myself under a
strain. I admit that. I didn't like dissection, I didn't
like the damaged human stuff in the wards. Some
of it was pitiful; some of it horrified me."

I agreed with him. "Doctoring has always ter-
rified *me*. *I* couldn't stand any of it."

"But the world must have doctors," he said.

"It won't have *me* for a doctor. I've never seen
more than three dead people, and they were all
lying quietly laid out in bed."

"But on the road? You come upon dreadful
sights."

"We never travel by road. All sane people are
giving it up."

"You, I see, have avoided the ugly side of life
from the first. Well—I didn't. I walked right into
it when I chose medicine. I thought of the good
I could do and I never thought of the harsh red
realities I should have to face. You avoided. I tried
not to avoid and then I ran away. I went to that

district with the full idea of escape. This, I told myself, will be away from any war there is or any bombing. Here I can recover myself. Here, I said, there will be nothing except normal cases I can really face and help. Cainsmarsh is far from any main roads. There won't be even motor casualties, which are often so frightful to encounter. You see my point? It looked as good as any possible world for me, and going there in summertime with the wild flowers out and a hundred sorts of butterfly about, dragon-flies and an abundance of summer birds, let alone a lot of summer visitors, mostly houseboat and fishing people with children and their small ailments, there didn't seem to be very much wrong with it. I would have laughed if you had told me that I had come into a haunted land.

"I did all I could to protect myself from over-stimulation. I did not have a newspaper in the house. I relied on a weekly news summary with no illustrations but diagrams. I wouldn't open a book later than Dickens.

"The native population seemed at first just a trifle stupid and reserved but quite kindly. I saw nothing wrong with them to begin with. Old

Rawdon, the vicar of Cross in Slackness, that land-
mark church of the levels, told me that there was
a good deal of furtive drugging because of the
ague and that he suspected the genuineness of
their amiability. I went to pay my respects to him
as soon as I was able. He was an elderly man and
rather deaf and he had exchanged to the Cross
in Slackness living because of his infirmity. His
church and vicarage were stranded, so to speak,
with one or two cottages on a sort of crocodile
back of land, and they were overgrown with elm
trees. I doubt if even as many as a score of people
came to his services. He was not very communicative, his old bent wife was even less so, he had
trouble with gallstones and an ulcerated contu-
sion of the ankle, and his chief preoccupation
seemed to be with the high-church tendencies of
his fellow-priest, a newly arrived curate at Marsh
Havering. Apparently he himself was low church
and Calvinistic, but at first I could not understand the mixture of fear and resentment with
which he spoke of the younger man. There were
no landed gentry in Cainsmarsh, and, except for a
veterinary surgeon, a few elementary teachers, one
or two publicans, and some middle-class board-

ing-house keepers towards Beacon Ness, the population was entirely a population of farmers and farm workers. They had no folk-lore, no songs, no arts, and no special costume. A more improbable soil for anything you could call psychic it would be hard to imagine. And yet you know——"

He frowned and spoke in measured words, as if he was doing his utmost to be explicit and was reasoning against the possible objections I might presently make to what he had to tell me.

"After all . . . It is in just such a flat, still atmosphere perhaps—translucent, gentle-coloured—that things lying below the surface, things altogether hidden in more eventful and colourful surroundings, creep on our perceptions. . . ."

He paused, drank a glass of his wine, reflected for a moment, and resumed.

"There can be no disputing the stillness of that district. Sometimes I would stop my car on one of the winding dike roads and stand listening before I went on again. One would hear the sheep upon the lavender-coloured hills, four or five miles away, or the scream of some distant water fowl, like a long, harsh scratch of neon light across the silent blue, or the sound of the wind and the sea, a dozen miles away at Beacon Ness, like the world breathing in its sleep. At night of course there were more noises: dogs howled and barked in the distance, corncrakes called, and things rustled in the reeds. And yet the nights too could sometimes have a stillness. . . .

"At first it did not seem to be of any particular significance that the traceable consumption of soporifics and opiates by this apparently insensitive population was not only quite remarkably high but increasing, nor that the proportion of suicides and inexplicable crimes—inexplicable as distinguished from normally motivated offences—over this part of the world was exceptional and apparently rising. Dealing with such a small population, however, a murder more or less could upset the percentage altogether. Face to face in the daylight there was nothing at all murderous in the bearing of these people. They did not look you in the eye—but that may have been their idea of good manners. It just happened that there had been no less than three crazy murders of relations and neighbours in Cainsmarsh in the past five years, and of two of them the perpetrators were still undiscovered. The other was a fratricide. The vicar, when I spoke about this, said something about 'degenerate race—too inbred' and changed the subject, as though it was an unpleasant topic of no particular importance for him.

"The first real intimation I had in my own person, of the brooding strangeness that hangs over Cainsmarsh, was an attack of insomnia. Hitherto I had been a fairly sound sleeper but before I had settled in the Marsh for a couple of months my nights began to be troubled. I would wake up in a state of profound uneasiness, and without any physiological cause that I could trace I fell a prey to evil dreams. They were quite peculiar dreams, like none I had ever dreamt before. They were dreams of menace, of being waylaid, stalked, and pursued and of furious struggles to defend myself, dreams out of which I would wake shouting— you know those faint shadowy shouts of dreamland conflicts—sweating and trembling in every limb. Some of these dreams had so strong a flavour of horror that they would leave me afraid to go to sleep again. I would try to read, and whatever I read in the night watches an eerie discomfort hung over me.

"I adopted all the expedients that would naturally occur to a young medical man to end these enervating experiences, but without avail. I dieted. I exercised. I would get up and dress, go out either on foot or in my car, in spite of a strong fear resistance. Fear pursued me out of those dreams. The nightmare quality hung about me and could not be shaken off. I was awake and still dreaming. Never have I seen such sinister skies as I did on those night excursions. I felt such a dread of unfamiliar shadows as I had not known even in childhood. There were times on those nocturnal drives when I could have shouted aloud for daylight as a man suffocating in a closed chamber might shout for air.

"Very naturally this inability to sleep began presently to undermine my daily life. I became nervous and fanciful. I found I was giving way to minor hallucinations, rather, I suppose, after the pattern of delirium tremens. But with more menace in them. I would turn convulsively under the impression that a silent hound was creeping up to attack me from behind, or I would imagine a black snake wriggling out from under the valance of an arm-chair.

"Presently came other symptoms of relaxing mental control. I found myself suspecting the Island doctors of a combination against me. The most petty incidents, small slights, breaches of etiquette, fancied imputations, had been seized upon by my imagination and worked up into the fabric of a conspiracy mania. I had to restrain myself from writing foolish letters or making challenges and asking questions. Then I began to find something evil in the silence or in the gestures of some of my patients. And while I sat by their bedsides, I fancied that there were hostile goings-to-and-fro and malignant whisperings and conspirings just outside the door.

"I could not understand what was the matter with me. I searched my mind for nervous stresses and I could find none. I had surely left all that behind in London. Temperature and so forth remained normal. But clearly there was something askew in my adjustment to these new surroundings. Cainsmarsh was disappointing my expectations. There was no healing in it for me. I had to pull myself together. I had sunk all my little capital in the practice and I had to stick it. There was nowhere else for me to go. I had to keep my head and grapple with this trouble and beat it before it became too much for me.

"Was it just my own trouble? Was something specially wrong with me or was it something wrong with the countryside? Were there other people in the Marsh having dreams and fancies like mine, or maybe was this a trouble that came to newcomers and passed away? Was it something I should get over? A sort of acclimatization. I had to be careful with my inquiries because it is not well for a doctor to admit he is out of sorts. I began to watch my patients, my old servant, and anyone with whom I came in contact for any betrayal of symptoms similar to mine. And I found what I looked for. Beneath the superficial stolidity a number of these people were profoundly uneasy. There was fear in the Marsh for them as for me. It was an established habitual fear. But it was not a definite fear. They feared something unknown. It was a sort of fear that might concentrate at any time upon anything whatever and transform it into a thing of terror.

"Let me give you some instances.

"One evening I found an old lady stiff with dread at a shadow in a corner, and when I moved her candle and the shadow moved, she screamed aloud. 'But it can't hurt you,' I argued. 'I'm afraid,' she answered, as though that was a sufficient answer. And suddenly before I could prevent her she had seized a little clock on the night table beside her and flung it at that dark and dreadful nothingness, and buried her head under the clothes. I will confess that for a moment or so I stood rigid and expectant staring at the broken clock in the corner.

"And one day I saw a farmer who was rabbit shooting pause, stare aghast at a fluttering scarecrow, and then, unaware of my presence, suddenly raise his gun and blow the poor dangling old rapscallion to bits.

"There was an unusual terror of the dark. My old servant, I found, would not venture out after twilight to the pillar box a hundred yards away. She would make every sort of excuse and when she was cornered she refused absolutely to go. I had to go myself or leave my letters until the morning. Even sweethearting, I learnt, would not tempt the young people abroad after sundown.

"I can't tell you," he said, "how the perception of the presence of fear grew upon me and grew upon me—how it infected me—until at last the flap of a window blind in the breeze or the fall of a cinder in the fireplace would set my nerves aquiver.

"I could not shake this off; my nights got worse. I determined to have a real talk about this queer uneasiness of the mind, with the old vicar. In his way, you see, the district was his business, as in my way it was mine. He ought to know whatever was to be known. By this time the disorder was getting a strong hold upon me. I made up my mind to go to him after a night of exceptional horror and dismay. I was indeed already pretty bad. . . .

"I can recall here and now the unprotected feeling of my drive to him across the open marshes. They seemed to me far too open, bare to endless dangers. And yet when I came near a clump of trees or bushes it took on the quality of an ambush. The normal confidence of a living creature was deserting me. I felt not simply exposed to incalculable evils, I felt threatened by them. In broad daylight, mind you; in the sunshine. With nothing but a few birds in sight. . . .

"As it happened I caught the old man in a communicative mood. I put my questions plainly to him. 'I'm a newcomer in this country,' I said. 'Is there something—something *peculiarly* wrong about it?'

"He stared at me and scratched his cheek, weighing what he should tell me. 'Yes,' he said, 'there is.'

"He led me into his study, listened for a moment as if to make sure that everyone was out of earshot, and then closed the door carefully. 'You're sensitive,' he said. 'You're getting it sooner than I did. Something—wrong—wrong and getting worse. Something evil.'

"I remember those opening words very plainly and his bleary old eyes and the bad teeth in his sagging mouth. He came and sat down quite close to me with one long bony hand cupping his hairy ear. 'Don't speak too loud,' he said. 'If you speak distinctly, I can hear.'

"He said he was glad to have someone to talk

it over with at last. He told me how he had hoped to end his days in the Marsh quietly and how gradually this shadowy discomfort had come over him, deepening slowly into fear. He could never afford another exchange. He too was fixed. It was hard to talk about. His wife would never talk to him about it. Before they came to Cross in Slackness, they had been the best of friends and gossips. 'Now,' he said, 'it is pushing us apart. I have to talk to myself. I don't know what's come over her.'

"'What is pushing you apart?' I asked.

"'The Evil.'

"That was his name for it.

"Everyone, he said, was being pushed apart. You began to find sinister possibilities in the most ordinary relations. Lately he had had a curious suspicion of his food—had fancied a queer taste in it and queer feelings after it. 'It makes me fear for my reason,' he said. 'My reason or hers.' Yet all the same, it was queer about the food. Why should anyone—? He left it at that. At his first coming the common people had seemed simply dull to him. Then he had begun to realize that they were not so much dull as reserved and suspicious. You would catch a glance in their eyes like a dog that may snap. Even the children, when you came to watch them, were furtively defensive. For no reason. For no reason at all. He told me that, sitting very close to me, not speaking too loud.

"He came closer. 'They are cruel to animals,' he told me. 'They beat their dogs and horses. Not regularly. By fits.

"'The children come to school with marks on them,' he said. . . . 'You can't get them to say anything. . . . They are afraid.'

"I asked him if he felt that this thing, whatever it was, was increasing. Had it always been there? There was very little recorded history of the region. He thought it was increasing. Things had not always been like this. I suggested that it may have always been in the atmosphere of the place and that we became more aware of it as we fell under the spell.

"'Maybe. Partly that,' said the old vicar.

"He gave some broken fragments of a story about a former incumbent. He and his wife had been sent to prison for cruelty to a servant girl. Prison! They said she told lies and had dirty habits. As an excuse. They wanted to cure her, they said. But really they just hated her. . . . Never anything against them before they came into the Marsh.

"'It's always been here,' whispered the old vicar. 'Always. Below the surface. An unhappy, wicked spirit that creeps into us all. I pray. I do not know what would happen to me if I did not pray. What with the waste of money and the rudeness of everybody and the malicious mischief they do me and the stone-throwing. Let alone the poison. It is the poisoning hurts me most.'

"We talked like that in his big shabby, sparely furnished study in the broad daylight, like men who cower in a cave.

"And then he began to talk less sanely. The evil was in the soil, he declared, *underground*. He laid great stress on the word 'underground.' He made a downward gesture with his quivering hand. There was something mighty and dreadful, buried in Cainsmarsh. Something colossally evil. Broken up. Scattered all over the Marsh. 'I think I know what it is,' he whispered darkly, but for a time he would not explain.

"They kept on stirring it up, he said, they would not let it rest.

"Whom did he mean by *they*? That was difficult. There had been road-making, there have been drainage works and now 'those archæologists'! And that was not all. There had been a ploughing of old pastures during the war. Opening old sores. 'You see over all the place was once a wilderness of graves.'

"'Tumuli?' I questioned.

"'No,' he insisted. 'Graves—graves everywhere!' And some of the ancient people, he said, were 'petrified.' You found stones of the strangest shapes. Abominable shapes. 'They keep on bringing things up,' he said. 'Things that had better be let alone. Ought to be let alone. Making doubts and puzzles—destroying faith.'

"At a jump he was denouncing Darwinism and evolution. It was remarkable how life-long controversies had interwoven with his Cainsmarsh distresses! Had I seen the museum at Eastfolk? he asked.

"He talked of the great bones exhibited there. But I protested he was thinking of the bones of

mammoths and dinosaurs and suchlike things.
Giants, he insisted. Look at what they call implements there! Too big and clumsy for any living
man to handle. Axes, spears—nothing but huge
weapons for killing and killing! '*Murder stones*'
he called them. The murder stones of giants.

"He clenched his bony fist, his quavering voice
rose, and real hatred came into his eyes.

"'Nothing is too bad,' he said, 'for the men
who dig up those bones. Tearing up dark secrets.
Seeming to confute. . . . A grave's a grave and a
dead man's a dead man, even if he's been dead a
million years. Let the evil creatures lie! Let them
lie! Let their dust lie!' He ceased to be furtively
confidential; his anger rose and thrust his fear
aside. He no longer troubled to listen to anything
I had to say in reply to him.

"He was soon launched upon the wildest dia-
tribe. He was transfigured by an anger that shook
his feeble frame. He had fixed upon the local
archæologists and naturalists as the chief objec-
tive for his tirade, but mixed up with that in the
oddest and most illogical way was his detestation of the high-church practices that had been
introduced by the new man at Marsh Havering.

Just when this Evil was being released and rising like an exhalation from the earth, when the one supreme need of the time was religion straight and stern—'*straight and stern*,' he repeated and shook his fingers in my face—this man must come with his vestments and images and music and mummery!

"But I will not give you, if I could, an imitation of that poor old wreck as he grew fiercer and louder and hoarser. He wanted suppression, he wanted persecution of Science, of Rome, of every sort of immorality and immodesty, of every sort of creed except his own, persecution, enforced repentance, to save us from the Wrath that was coming steadily upon us. 'They turn up the soil, they strip things bare, and we breathe the dust of long-dead men.' It was as if he was trying to escape from our common marshland obsession by sheer screaming violence. 'The doom of Cain!' he shouted. 'The punishment of Cain!'

"'But *why* Cain?' I managed to insert.

"'He ended his days here,' the old man declared. 'Oh, I know! Is this called Cainsmarsh for nothing? He wandered over the face of the earth and at last he came here, he and the worst of his sons. They poisoned the earth. Age after age of crime and cruelty, and then the Flood buried them under these marshes—and there they ought to be buried for ever.'

"I tried to argue against this fantasy—Cainsmarsh is just a corruption of Gaynes Marsh, as all the guide books say; it is written Gaynes in Domesday Book—but the old man bore me down. My voice had no chance now amidst his croaking assertions. His deafness was a shield against all argument. His voice filled the room. He poured out the festering accumulations of his brooding solitude. His sentences had the readiness of long-matured expression. I guess most of it had been uttered, time and again, to the faithful remnant of Cross in Slackness church. He had got the children of Cain and the cave men and the mammoths and megatheria and dinosaurs all jumbled up in the wildest confusion. It was a storm of preposterous nonsense. And yet—and yet, you know——"

Dr. Finchatton regarded the bay of Les Noupets in silence for a few moments.

"Out of it all came a suggestion. I doubt if it will seem even remotely sane to you—in this clear air. But it was the suggestion that this haunting something was something remote, archaic, bestial. . . ."

He nodded his head in doubtful confirmation of what he was saying.

"You see . . . It's bad enough to be haunted by Georgian ghosts, Stuart ghosts, Elizabethan ghosts, ghosts in armour and ghosts in chains. Yet anyhow, one has a sort of fellow-feeling for them. They aren't just spirits of cruelty, suspicion, and ape-like malice. But the souls of a tribe of cave men might be. . . . Grisly ghosts. . . . What do *you* think?"

"One may be as possible as the other," I said.

"Yes. And yet, if cave men, why not apes? Suppose all our ancestors rose against us! Reptiles, fish, amœbæ! The idea was so fantastic that, as I drove away from Cross in Slackness, I tried to laugh."

Dr. Finchatton stopped short and looked at me. "*I couldn't laugh,*" he said.

"I don't think *I* could have done," I said. "It's a frightful idea. I'd rather be haunted by a man than an ape any day."

"I drove back home more saturated with terror

than I came. I was beginning to see visions now everywhere. There was an old man bending down in a ditch doing something to a fallen sheep and he became a hunched, bent, and heavy-jawed savage. I did not dare look to see what he was doing and, when he called something to me— maybe only a good-day-to-you—I pretended not to hear. Whenever a clump of bushes came near the road, my heart sank and I slackened pace and, as soon as I was past, I jammed down the accelerator.

"I got drunk, Sir, for the first time in my life that night. You see, it was either getting drunk or running away. Maybe I'm still a young doctor, but that's my code. A doctor who quits his practice without notice is as bad as a sentinel who bolts. So you see, I had to get drunk.

"Before I went to bed I found I was funking opening the front door to look out. So with a convulsive effort I flung it open wide. . . .

"There crouched the marshes under the moonlight and the long low mists seemed to have stayed their drifting at the slam of the door against the wall. As if they paused to listen. And over it all was something, a malignant presence such as I had never apprehended before.

"Nevertheless I stuck to my doorstep. I did not retreat. I attempted even a drunken speech.

"I forget what I said. Maybe I myself went far enough back to the Stone Age to make mere inarticulate sounds. But the purport was defiance —of every evil legacy the past has left for man."

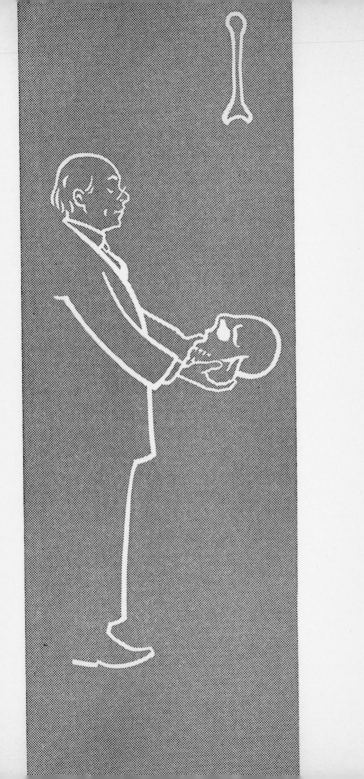

The
Skull in the
Museum

At this point in his narrative Dr. Finchatton stopped abruptly. "This sounds a crazy story to you?" he said. "Do you want me to go on with it?"

"Not in the least," I spluttered. "I mean, yes, please. I mean, do *please* go on. I'm tremendously interested. But sitting here at this table with everything bright and clear and definite, there is a certain unreality . . . If you understand me?"

"*I* understand you," he said without returning my smile. He looked round. "It does seem here as though nothing except vermouth and seltzer and lunchtime presently, and things like that, could ever happen any more."

A look of extreme weariness came over him.

"I'm resting," he said. "Yes. But sooner or later I shall have to go back to it all. I'd like to go on talking about it a bit—to you. If you don't mind. There's something—if I might say so—so refreshingly unimaginative about you. Like white paper."

At the time I was quite prepared to go on listening. I was oblivious then of the possibility that this story might ever disturb my own slumbers. I keep dreams for waking moments but I like them then. Fancies and reveries. I welcome them. One dreams then but one feels quite safe. There may be shivers in it but no real fear. It is just because they *are* impossible that I like impossible stories. Ever since I discovered Edgar Allan Poe in my early boyhood I have had a taste for the weird and the eerie, and in spite of my aunt's opposition—she flies into a regular passion at the suggestion that anything irregular or unusual can ever occur—I have—in an unobtrusive way—indulged it pretty freely. Her imagination, I think, was killed long ago, but mine I've made into a domestic pet that I like to play with. I do not think it will ever claw me seriously; it's a pussy now which knows where to stop. Though I am not so sure of that as I was. But it was very pleasant to be there, safe and solid, in the clear Normandy sunshine, and hear about those terror-stricken marshes. "Go on, my dear Sir," said I. "Go on."

"Well," said Dr. Finchatton, "I put up as much fight as my training and quality permitted. Getting drunk and that speech of defiance, even if in fact I imagined it rather than made it, did me good. I slept that night, good forgetful sleep, for the first time for weeks, and next day rose refreshed to reckon with my situation. Trained as I was, it was natural for me to assume that this common ailment of fear and fantasy, this sickness of a whole region, must be due to some virus in the air or the water or the soil. I made a private resolution to drink water only after it had been boiled and eat only well-cooked food. But also I was quite open to the idea that something less material might be at work. I am no prejudiced materialist. I was quite prepared to believe in purely psychic infection—though not of course in these Sons of Cain of the vicar's. I decided next morning that I would investigate that high-church curate at Marsh Havering, the Reverend Mortover, the object of the vicar's peculiar detestation, and find what *he* might have to say about it.

"But I found the young man as mad as his Calvinistic colleague. If the old man mixed the trouble up with science and excavations and Romanism, the young man blamed the Reformation and made great play with the Puritan witch mania of the sixteenth century. Some spiritual control was broken then, he assured me with the utmost confidence. Diabolism had returned to the earth. It was not the ghost of Cain and his wicked sons that was troubling us, according to him; it was diabolical possession. We have to restore the unity of Christendom and exorcize these devils.

"He was a very pale, clean-shaven young man, with a fine clear-cut face, burning dark eyes, and high-pitched tenor voice. He made few gestures and he kept his thin hands clenched as he talked. If he had been in the Roman Catholic Church instead of being just a high Anglican, they would have set him to conduct missions. He had just that sort of eloquent intensity. And there he sat in his cassock, looking up and away over my shoulder and expounding the exorcism of the marshes.

"As he talked I could see that his head was full of long, slow processions winding across the marshes with banners, canopies, vestments, boys chanting, censers swinging, priests asperging. I thought of the old vicar peering out of his dirty study window and I had a vision of him running out hoarse and stumbling, with murder in his eyes.

"'But,' I told him, 'there will be opposition!' and at that the manner of Mr. Mortover changed. He stood up and threw out a stiff hand like an eagle's claw. 'It must be overcome!' said he, and in that instant I understood why men are killed in Belfast and Liverpool and Spain."

That was queer. I interrupted. "But, Dr. Finchatton, what have Belfast and Liverpool and Spain to do with Cainsmarsh?" I asked.

That brought him to a stop for a moment. He looked at me with a very peculiar expression, something between suspicious scrutiny and obstinacy. "I was talking of Cainsmarsh," he said after deliberation.

"Then what have Belfast and Spain to do with it?"

"Nothing. I mentioned them, I suppose—by way of illustration. . . . Let me get it! Let me get it! What I was thinking of was fanaticism. Both these men, the vicar and the priest, had their convictions—yes. High and noble convictions, no doubt, as they professed them. But what they really wanted to do was to fight. They wanted to be at each other's throats. That was where the haunting poison of the Marsh came in. It wasn't their beliefs that stirred them; it was their fears. He wanted to shout and provoke. . . .

"Well—so for that matter did I. Why had I bawled and raved at the Marsh out of my door over night? And shaken my fist?"

He looked at me almost as if he expected me to answer.

"The Greeks had a word for it," he said. "Panic. Endemic panic, that was the contagion of the marshes."

"That may be a name for it," I said. "But how much does that explain?"

"You realize," said Dr. Finchatton, "that by this time I was in a headlong panic against panic. I felt that my time was running short. If I did not

do something to exorcize it, the spirit of the
Marsh would get me—surely. I should break. I
should do something violent. I happened to have
nothing very pressing just then to tie me, and I
determined to play hookey from my consulting
room for half a day and go over to Eastfolk museum. I would have a good reassuring look at
those mammoth bones, which under the vicar's
suggestion were beginning to take on far too human a form in my memory, and perhaps have a
chat with the curator, who, I had heard, was an
archæologist of considerable ability.

"I found him a very pleasant little man, with
a broad bland bare face and spectacles and a sort
of watchfulness. He had that sort of watchfulness
good photographers and portrait painters have,
and it was the only thing that was not altogether
comfortable about him. I caught him looking at
me whenever I turned away from him. . . .

"I professed a great interest in the flint implements which are so abundant in the low hills
above the marshlands and about the series of human remains that had been unearthed there. He
was an enthusiast and he found me intelligent.

He embarked upon quite a history of the region. 'It must have been inhabited,' I said, 'for thousands of years.'

"'Hundreds of thousands,' he told me. 'There were Neanderthalers and— But let me show you our special glory!'

"He led me to a locked glass cupboard in which was a thick louring beetle-browed skull, that still seemed to scowl from its empty sockets. Beside it was its under jaw. This dirty rusty-brown treasure, he said, was the completest specimen of its kind in the world. It was almost unbroken. It had already settled a dozen controversies arising out of the fragmentary nature of its fellows. There were also a few vertebræ from the neck and a curved thigh bone and a lot of smaller fragments in a case close by, but the entire fissure in which these remains had been found had not yet been cleaned up, because the bones were half dissolved and very brittle and had to be extracted very carefully. The fissure was being worked with elaborate care. In the end they hoped to get almost an entire skeleton. Two or three very primitive and clumsy artifacts had also been found in this same cleft in the chalk, down which maybe the brute had slipped and been jammed and covered up. The little curator watched me as I surveyed his prize specimen and marked the snarling grin of its upper jaw and the shadowy vitality that still lurked in the caverns whence its eyes had once glared upon the world.

"'That might, I suppose, be our ancestor?' I said.

"'More probable than not.'

"'That in our blood!' I said.

"I turned half round and looked at the monster askance and, when I spoke again, I spoke as if he also might be listening. I asked a score of amateurish questions. There had been countless generations of him and his kind, I learnt. His sort had slouched and snarled over the marshes for a hundred times the length of all recorded history. In comparison with *his* overlordship our later human rule was a thing of yesterday. Millions of these brutish lives had come and passed, leaving fragments, implements, stones they had chipped or reddened by their fires, bones they had gnawed. Not a pebble in the marsh, not an inch of ground, their feet had not pressed or their hands gripped a myriad times.

"'Just something a little bit dreadful about him,' I said, talking vacuously while I made up my mind. Then I decided to put a question point-blank. I asked the curator had he heard—had he ever met the idea that the Marsh was haunted?

"The scrutiny in the magnified eyes behind the glasses intensified. He had heard something.

"'*Well?*' said I.

"But he wanted me to speak first. He waited silently, and so I was forced to go on. I told him practically all that I have told you. 'The marshes have got hold of me,' I said. 'And if I do not do something about it, they will drive me mad. I can't stand them and I have to stand them. Tell me why it is one dreams there so dismally, why one is haunted by fear in the daylight and horrible fears in the night?'

"'You're not the first who has come to me with that question,' he said, still watching me.

"'And you can tell me,' I said, 'what it is?'

"'No,' he said.

"He was a careful man with his words as well as a watchful one with his eyes. He explained he went into the marsh to excavate and so he saw something of the people. 'They don't like these excavations,' he said. 'I have never heard of so much distrust of digging in any other part of the world. Maybe it is a strong local superstition. Maybe fear is contagious. They certainly fear. And I think they fear more today than they used to do. It is often very hard now to get permission to dig on private land.'

"I could see he was not telling me all he had in mind. He seemed to be saying things to me experimentally, as if he was trying out his ideas on me. He remarked that he never slept in the marsh even in the daytime. At times when he was sifting earth he would stop to listen, and resume sifting, and then stop still again. 'Nothing to hear,' he said, 'and yet one gets strung up like that.'

"He came to a pause. I saw him looking very hard and with a peculiar expression at the cave man's skull against the wall between us.

"'You don't think an ugly beast like that could really leave a ghost?' I asked.

"'It's left its bones,' he said. 'Do you think it had anything you could call a spirit? Something that might still be urgent to hurt and torment and frighten? Something profoundly suspicious and easily angered?'

"It was my turn to stare at him.

"'You do not really believe that. You are suggesting that to me. For some purpose.'

"He laughed, still with a steady eye on me. 'If so, I have failed,' he said. 'But I did want to suggest it to you. If we can make a ghost of this fear of yours—well, ghosts can be laid. If we make a fever of it, fever can be cured. But while this remains merely panic fear and a smouldering rage, what can we do about it?'

"'Very kind of you,' said I, 'to try and pull me together in that fashion, truss my mind, so to speak, for exorcism. It isn't so easy as that.'

"And then," said Dr. Finchatton, "he switched off that hypnotic bespectacled stare of his and began to talk to me more frankly.

"What he said was rather metaphysical," Dr. Finchatton said, "and I am not much of a metaphysician. It was queer theoretical stuff and yet, in a way, it had a sort of air of explanation. I will try and tell it you as well as I can. The expression he used was that we were breaking the frame of our present—the Frame of our Present?"

Dr. Finchatton looked at me inquiringly. I remained judicial. I had not the remotest idea what the frame of our present might be. "Go on," I said.

"He stood with his profile to me, no longer watching me, looking out of the window and saying what was in his mind. 'A century or so ago,' he said, 'men lived in the present far more than they do now. Their past went back four or five thousand years, their future hardly went as far, they lived for *now*. And what they called the eternities. They knew nothing of the remote real past. They cared nothing for the real future. *That*' —and he nodded at the cave man's skull—'just wasn't there. All that was buried and forgotten and out of life. We lived in a magic sphere and we felt taken care of and safe. And now in the last century or so, we have broken that. We have poked into the past, unearthing age after age, and we peer more and more forward into the future. And that's what's the matter with us.'

"'In the Marsh?' said I.

"'Everywhere. Your vicar and priest know that by instinct though they don't know how to express it—or anyhow they don't express it as you and I do. Sometimes it's nearer the surface in the Marsh—but it's everywhere. We have broken the frame of the present and the past, the long black past of fear and hate that our grandfathers never knew of, never suspected, is pouring back upon us. And the future opens like a gulf to swallow us up. The animal fears again and the animal rages again and the old faiths no longer restrain it. The cave man, the ancestral ape, the ancestral brute, have returned. So it is. I can assure you I am talking realities to you. It is going on now everywhere. You have been in the Marsh. You have felt them in the Marsh, but I tell you these resurrected savageries are breathing now and thrusting everywhere. The world is full of menace—not only here.' He stopped short and his spectacles flashed as he looked at me and then stared again out of the window.

"'But,' said I, 'this is all very fine and mystical but how does it help me? What am I to do?'

"He said this was a mental thing and it had to be fought out in the mind.

"'I have to go back to the Marsh this evening.'

"He went on saying that the frame of the present was shattered and could never be restored. I had to open out—'open out,' he said—and enlarge my mind to a vaster world where the cave man was as present as the daily paper and a thousand years ahead was on the doorstep. 'That is all very well,' I said, 'but what does it mean? What am *I* to do now? I am asking you; what am *I* to do now?'

"His regard came back to me. 'Fight it out if you can,' he said. 'Go back. You won't escape by running away. Go back and have one more round with whatever you choose to fancy it, the Evil, the Fear, the Ghost of Cain, or *that* fellow's ghost——'

"He paused, and we both looked round at the clumsy skull as though we felt it might have something to say in the matter.

"'Broaden your mind to the new scale,' he resumed, rather more confidentially. 'Face it if you can. And then if you still find you are slipping, you must try to get help. You should go off to London and have a definite treatment. The man you should see is Norbert, of—I think it is

Harley Street, but I can get that for you. He has been one of the first men to realize this spreading miasma of the mind of which you are suffering, and devise some sort of treatment for it. To tell you the truth, he has helped me. Though his methods are rough and strange. I had some slight touch of your trouble and, as I happened to know about him, I called him in. And early. He flies over to Les Noupets once or twice a week. There's a clinic over there. . . .'

"So much for the curator of the Eastfolk museum. For the time he pulled me together. His modern scientific lingo was something I could understand. I felt that I was no longer being hunted darkly and strangely and beyond any possibility of help; I was just an experimentalist facing a disagreeable and risky but by no means impossible challenge.

"But I had no luck in that last round with the ghosts of the cave men," said Dr. Finchatton. "I went back while it was still daylight. At the very outset before I reached my house I came upon something dreadful. It was a dog that had been beaten to death. Yes; beaten to death! You may think that in this world where so many terrible things are happening, a cruelly ill-treated dog was no great matter. It was to me.

"I saw it lying among the nettles by the roadside. I thought some motorist must have run over it and thrown it aside. I got down to look at it and make sure that it was dead. It wasn't simply dead; it was battered to a pulp. With some blunt heavy instrument. There couldn't have been a whole bone left in it. Somebody must have rained blows upon it, a frantic whirlwind of blows.

"For a medical man I know I am over-sensitive. At any rate I went on through the sunshine in a state of horror, at nature, at the deep fountains of cruelty in the human make-up. What frantic outburst had destroyed that poor brute? And then I had hardly been back in my house ten minutes when another shock arrived. This again may seem a small matter to you. To me it was overwhelming. A breathless messenger came on a bicycle from the vicarage of Cross in Slackness. He was so scared that for some moments I could not understand what he was telling me, and then I realized that old Rawdon had set upon his poor old wife and done his best to kill her. He had knocked her down and beaten her. 'The poor old lady!'

gasped the boy. 'You better come soon. We got him tied up in the outhouse and she's on the bed upstairs scared to death—too frightened to speak. He's raving something frightful. Frightful. Says she tried to poison him. . . . The language! . . .'

"I brought out my car again and went over. I managed what I could to make the poor old thing comfortable; he hadn't hurt her so much as I feared, a few bruises but no bones broken, and it was chiefly shock and amazement she suffered from; and presently two policemen came and carried off old Rawdon to the police station at Holdingham. I wouldn't go down to see him. She spoke just a word or two as she lay there. 'Edward!' she muttered and then in amazement: 'Oh, *Edward!*' And then sharply, with a note of terror: '*Edward!*' and a weak scream. I gave her a sleeping draught and arranged for a woman to stay the night with her and then I went back to my own place.

"So long as I was actively employed I kept going, but as soon as I got home I found myself slumping. I could eat nothing. I drank a lot of whisky and instead of going to bed I fell asleep in an arm-chair by the fire. I awoke in terror and found the fire nearly out. I went to bed, and when at last I got to sleep, the dreams closed in on me and I sat up again starkly awake. I got up and put on an old dressing gown and went downstairs and made up the fire, determined to keep awake at any cost. But I dozed there and then went back to bed. And so between the bed and the fireside I dragged through the night. My dreams were all a mix-up of the poor scared old lady, the almost as pitiful old man, the ideas the museum custodian had put in my head, and, brooding over it all, that infernal palæolithic skull.

"More and more did the threat of that primordial Adamite dominate me. I could not banish that eyeless stare and that triumphant grin from my mind, sleeping or waking. Waking I saw it as it was in the museum, as if it were a living presence that had set us a riddle and was amused to hear our inadequate attempts at a solution. Sleeping I saw it released from all rational proportions. It became gigantic. It became as vast as a cliff, a mountainous skull in which the orbits and hollows of the jaw were huge caves. He had an effect—it is hard to convey these dream effects

—as if he were continually rising and yet always towering there. In the foreground I saw his innumerable descendants, swarming like ants, swarms of human beings hurrying to and fro, making helpless gestures of submission or deference, resisting an overpowering impulse to throw themselves under his all-devouring shadow. Presently these swarms began to fall into lines and columns, were clad in uniforms, formed up and began marching and trotting towards the black shadows under those worn and rust-stained teeth. From which darkness there presently oozed something —something winding and trickling, and something that manifestly tasted very agreeably to him. Blood."

And then Finchatton said a queer thing. "Little children killed by air-raids in the street."

I made no comment. I remained quietly attentive. It was an "aside," as actors used to say. He took up his story where he had left it.

"Morning," he resumed after an introspective pause, "found me frantic at the telephone. At great pains and what I am afraid will prove ruinous expense to me I managed to secure a locumtenens and forthwith I bolted off to London, gripping my sanity, so to speak, with both hands, to see this man Norbert. And it is Norbert who has sent me here. . . . Norbert, you know, is a very extraordinary man. He was not at all what I had expected."

Dr. Finchatton stopped short. He looked at me. "That's all."

I nodded silently.

"Well," he said, "what do you make of it?"

"In a day or so, perhaps, I shall begin to think something about it. At present I don't know what to say. It's incredible and yet—you almost make me believe it. I mean I don't think it really happened—I wouldn't go so far as that—but I believe it happened to you."

"Exactly. I'm glad to be able to talk to a man like you. It's what Norbert wants me to do. He wants me to familiarize myself with what has just happened to me, just in the spirit in which you have taken it, so as to be able to distinguish between the realities of my experience, the realities of life, he calls them, and the fears and fancies and dreams I have wrapped about them. His idea is that I ought to see things *unfeelingly*. Because after all—what do you think?" He looked at me very earnestly.

"How much of what I have been telling you is actual concrete happening and how much—what shall I call it?—mental reaction? Old Rawdon attacking his wife—that was real. That broken-up dog was real. . . . Norbert's idea, you know, is that I should talk it quietly over with anyone who —who seems reasonably balanced and not too worried about the past or the future. So as to get these facts as facts and not as dreads and horrors. He wants to bring me back, so to speak, to what he calls a rational insensitiveness—rational insensitiveness, that's his formula—and so get a firmer foothold for—whatever I have to do next."

He gulped down his wine. "It's very good of you to have listened to me," he said and then, as a shadow fell across the terrace before us: "*Hullo!*"

The Intolerable
Psychiatrist

I disliked the shadow of Dr. Norbert even before I looked up and saw him. He was and he meant to be an overwhelming sort of man and, though I am indolent, self-indulgent, and unenterprising, I can be as obstinate as a whole team of mules. I braced myself for opposition to whatever he wanted or had to say before he opened his mouth.

He was not at all the sort of person I should have expected a psychotherapeutist to be. A psychotherapeutist, I think, ought to have calm eyes and a reassuring manner—and a certain general neatness of self-control. He ought to look fresh and healthy, and this fellow was distinctly cadaverous. He was large and expansive and untidy with lots of undisciplined black hair and thick eyebrows, and his large dark and flashing eyes either rolled about in his more voluble moments or came to a focus in a dramatic pause and glared at you—not a steady look but a glare that pushed at your face and was supported by an immense frown. His features were uniformly large, and he had the loose mouth of an orator and a voice of remarkable amplitude. He wore an old-fashioned upstanding white collar and a loose black bow tie very much under one ear. It was as if he had dressed himself once for all in some remote pre-war fashion and never changed it since. He looked much more like an actor on vacation than a psychotherapeutist. He made me think of the old *Punch* pictures of the Grand Old Man, or Henry Irving, or Thomas Carlyle. A more unsuitable figure to interrupt a couple of decent-looking modern Englishmen sitting over their apéritifs on the terrace of the Perona Source Hotel it would be hard to imagine.

But there he was, entirely unlike anything I could have foreseen, the great Dr. Norbert, Finchatton's mental healer, hands on hip, looking down on me in his most impressive manner. Finchatton had described him as unexpected but the last thing

I should have expected was anything so large, so oracular, and so antique.

"I have been watching you from above," he said as though he were God Almighty. "I didn't want to interrupt while Finchatton was telling his tale. But now I perceive you have got through with it and I pounce."

Finchatton looked at me with a sort of silent entreaty to bear with Norbert's extraordinary manner and hear him out.

"You've heard his story?" Norbert demanded of me.

His manner did nothing to veil the fact that he was the psychotherapeutist and Finchatton was his "case." "He told you about how the cave man dawned upon his mind? He talked about that terror in Cainsmarsh? Good! And the growing realization of evil? Well—how have you reacted to that? What do you, with your manifestly very normal mind, make of it?"

He thrust his great face, all interrogation, some inches towards me. "Tell me in your own words," he said, and waited like a teacher examining a child.

"Dr. Finchatton," said I, "has been relating

some very extraordinary things. Yes. But I should
have to think them over a lot before I could pass
judgment upon them."

Norbert made the grimace of a teacher dealing
with a stupid child.

"But *I* want your reactions now. Before you
think."

"You *may* want," said I to myself. "I can't,"
I said aloud.

"But it will be of very great importance to Dr.
Finchatton for you to tell me now. Never mind
why."

Suddenly I heard a clock striking. "Good heav-
ens!" I cried, standing up and throwing a ten-
franc note to the hovering waiter. "I shall keep
my aunt waiting for lunch! That will *never*
do."

"But you *can't* leave this business like this!"
said Norbert featuring an incredulous amazement.
"You can't. It's your duty to a fellow-creature in
trouble to hear this case out and help to rational-
ize it. You *must* help us." Glare. "Positively I *can't*
release you."

I turned to Finchatton. "If Dr. Finchatton," I
said, "would like to talk about it some more . . ."

"Of course he wants to talk to you some more."

I kept my eyes on Finchatton, who nodded with an intensified appeal.

"I'll come again," I said. "Tomorrow. About this time. But I can't stay now. . . . It's impossible."

I went down the winding road at something between a walk and a trot—really concerned to be so late, because, you know, my aunt is simply awful if anyone keeps her waiting for lunch. I was already doubtful about the promise I had given and a little angry at having been forced to make it. It was as if I had admitted some preposterous claim upon my attention and had bought myself off.

I turned my head and saw the two men among those above me, side by side, Norbert overshadowing Finchatton.

"Tomorrow," I called—though I suppose I was well out of earshot.

Norbert made a large gesture.

Now I did not want in the least to see this Dr. Norbert any more. I had indeed conceived a violent antipathy for him. I did not like his "You-and-Finchatton-are-rabbits-and-now-I-am-

going-to-dissect you" style. I did not like his large
enveloping voice nor the way his brow and purpose seemed to overhang the rest of him. And I
detest angular commanding gestures made with
arms that are much too long. But on the other
hand I had taken a real liking to Dr. Finchatton
and developed a very lively interest in his story.
I thought he had told it very vividly. I wish I
could convey the conviction of his manner in this
transcript. Directly I got away from him I began
to think of questions I might have asked him and
to want to see him again. I regarded Norbert as a
nuisance who had just butted in upon an inter-
esting tale. I dismissed Norbert from my mind
and went on thinking of Finchatton.

There was something about this story of a magic
marshland into which a man might go, sane and
confident, admiring the butterflies and the flowers, and out of which presently he would come
running again frantic with fear and rage, that had
seized hold upon my imagination very strongly.
And the way in which that evil old skull, that
ancestral skull, lurking unseen at first in the background, had slowly become visible . . . ! It was

like something being lit up behind a transparency. It was an explanation that was itself an enigma. And now, degree by degree, those bare jaws were being clad and covered until a phantom lip framed the grinning teeth, and there were dark aggressive blood-shot eyes below the beetling brows. The cave man was becoming more and more plainly a living presence as the story germinated in my mind.

It was a face at last and not a skull that watched me out of that dream story. It was absurd, but indeed it seemed to be watching me. It watched me all that evening and it mopped and mowed in the night. It made me inattentive so that in the afternoon my combinations at croquet were unusually shortsighted and poor, and in the evening I offended my aunt deeply by failing to play up to my usual form. She was against me but, as she reckoned on my playing up to my usual form, she was surprised and perplexed by the things I did, and put quite off her game, so that she and her partner lost heavily. But I scarcely heeded her reproaches and I undressed slowly, my mind full of that distant marshland so mysteriously accursed, so monstrously overshadowed now by that brutish revenant. I sat for quite a long time thinking it over before I went to bed.

Next day I got up to the Perona Source Hotel rather late. I had meant to be early. I would have taken a tram but an *agent* explained they were not running. There had been a lightning strike organized by the Communists and there had been a fight at the depot in which several people had been injured."One must be firm these days," said the *agent*. Consequently I had to walk the whole way. And it was bad luck, I thought, to find Dr. Norbert stretching out his long legs under a table umbrella on the terrace and no signs of Dr. Finchatton. Norbert motioned for me to join him, and I sat down on a green chair beside his table. I did so reluctantly. I wanted to make it plain that it was Finchatton I wanted to see. I wanted more of the story and I did not want any mental probing, judgment, dissection, earnest invasion of my private thoughts by this pretentious individual.

"Where's your friend?" I asked.

"He cannot come down today. It is just as well."

"I thought he had arranged——"

"*He* thought he had arranged— But he was prevented. As I say, it is just as well."

"I don't see that."

"From *my* point of view. I want very much to get a common-sense outside view of this story that fills his mind. I want it for my own sake as well as his."

"But how can you expect me to contribute?"

"Well—for one simple thing: do you know any part of the world called Cainsmarsh?"

He turned round to look at me as he might have looked at an animal he had just given an injection.

"I imagined it was somewhere in fenland."

"There is no such district in the world."

"It is a pseudonym?"

"It is a myth."

He surveyed me for a moment and then decided that for the present I was not worth watching. He put his two long hands palm to palm in front of him and spoke with great deliberation, staring out to sea. "Our friend," he said, "*was* a doctor near Ely. Everything he told you was true and everything he told you was a lie. He is troubled beyond reason by certain things and the only way in which he can express them even to himself is by a fable."

"But some of these things—really happened?"

"Oh, yes. There *was* a case of gross cruelty to a dog. There *was* a poor old drunken parson who beat his wife. Things of that sort are happening all over the world every day. They are in the nature of things. If you cannot accept things like that, Sir, *you cannot live*. And Finchatton really went to the Tressider Museum at Ely, and Cunningham the custodian had the sense to spot his condition and send him on to me. But the mischief was already done to him before he went into the marsh. He's told you practically everything—but as though he showed it through bottle glass that distorted it all. And the reason why he has made it all up into that story . . ."

Dr. Norbert turned upon me, putting his arms akimbo and glaring at my face. He spoke with slow deliberation—as if he was speaking in capital letters: ". . . is because the realities that are overwhelming him are so monstrous and frightful that he has to transform them into this fairy tale about old skulls and silences in butterfly land, in the hope of getting them down to the dimensions of an hallucination and so presently expelling them from his thoughts."

The expression of his face made me uncomfortable. I turned and beckoned the waiter for another vermouth in order to recover my composure. "And what," I asked offhandedly, "may those more terrible realities be?"

"Do you never read a daily newspaper?" asked Dr. Norbert.

"Not very intently. Most of the stuff seems to me to be either pompous or wilfully disagreeable. But I do the *Times* Crossword Puzzle nearly every day. And I read most of the tennis and croquet stuff and so on. Have I missed much?"

"You've missed the things that have made Finchatton mad."

"Mad?"

"Didn't he repeat my phrase—endemic panic? A contagion in our atmosphere. A sickness in the very grounds of our lives, breaking out here and there and filling men's minds with a paralysing, irrational fear?"

"He did use that expression."

"Yes, Sir. And it is what I am dealing with here. It is what even I am only beginning to realize. A new plague—of the soul. A distress of the mind that has long lurked in odd corners of the mind, an endemic disorder, rising suddenly and spreading into a world epidemic. The story our friend put away into a sort of fairyland fenland is really the story of thousands of people today —and it will be the story of hundreds of thousands tomorrow. You are untroubled. As yet. . . . Maybe you are immune. . . . It is most important to me just now in my study of this increasing malaise that I should realize the reaction of an uninfected mind."

"I've never been good soil for out-of-the-way ideas," I said. "Still I don't want to take any risks. You don't think that presently I too shall begin to be frightened of the dark and scared in the open, and see ancestral apes and savages looming up over the world?"

He put his big hand across the table and pressed my arm for a moment. "If you do," he said, glaring portentously, "have courage."

It flashed into my mind abruptly that this man was really as mad as, or madder than, Finchatton. I put the question to him pat.

"Dr. Norbert, have *you* by any chance—got infected?"

The glare became intensified. He lifted up his face, so to speak, and then brought it down like a hammer on the word.

"Yes."

He spoke with such emphasis that my face was bedewed.

"I was an early case," he said. "I had to deal with myself. There was nobody to help me. I had to study myself. I have been through it all, Sir. And crawled out on the other side. A salted man, immunized. At the price of a monstrous struggle. . . ."

And with that he launched out upon the most astonishing dissertation I have ever heard. He made a little pause before the discourse came. What he had to say couldn't be said very well from a lounge chair. Presently he was sitting up and gripping his chair with both hands. Then he stood up and talked and walked about the terrace in front of me—no longer talking so much as orating. I have a fairly retentive memory, but it would be impossible for me now to give you a full report of all the strange tissue of assertion and arguments he poured forth. Some of his phrases and terms of thought I will quote. Finchatton's story had sounded like fantasy. This had no quality of fantasy about it at all. It began like pseudo-science and philosophy, but gradually it became more and more a booming, disconcerting exhortation. We were to take hold of life—*grip* it. Some of his ideas Finchatton had already handed on to me. I recognized the phrases. There was that about "breaking the Frame of the Present."

"But what does that *mean*?" I said almost irritably.

"Animals," he said, "live wholly in the present. They are framed in immediate things. So are really unsophisticated people. Israeli, Sands, Murphy, a crowd of people have been working on that." He rattled off a score of names but these are all that I remember. "But we men, we have been probing and piercing into the past and future. We have been multiplying memories, histories, traditions; we have filled ourselves with forebodings and plannings and apprehensions. And so our worlds have become overwhelmingly vast for us, terrific, appalling. Things that had seemed forgotten for ever have suddenly come back into the very present of our consciousness."

"In other words," said I, trying to keep him moored to current realities, "we have found out about the cave man."

"Found out about him!" he shouted. "We live in his presence. He has never died. He is anything but dead. Only . . ."

He came close and tapped my shoulder. ". . . only he was shut off from us and hidden. For a long time. And now we see him here face to face and his grin derides us. Man is still what he was. Invincibly bestial, envious, malicious, greedy. Man, Sir, unmasked and disillusioned, is the same fearing, snarling, fighting beast he was a hundred thousand years ago. These are no metaphors, Sir. What I tell you is the monstrous reality. The brute has been marking time and dreaming of a progress it has failed to make. Any archæologist will tell you as much; modern man has no better skull, no better brain. Just a cave man, more or less trained. There has been no real change, no real escape. Civilization, progress, all *that*, we are discovering, was a delusion. Nothing was secured. Nothing. For a time man built himself in, into his neat little *present* world of Gods and Providences, rainbow promises and so forth. It was artificial, it was artistic, fictitious. We are only beginning to realize *how* artificial. Now it is breaking down, Mr. Frobisher. It is breaking down all about us and we seem unable to prevent it. We *seem*. . . . No escape appears. No, Sir. Civilization so far has been a feeble, inadaptable falsity. And now it is found out; Fate has been too much for it. A stunning realization, Sir! And when sensitive, unprepared men like our poor friend Finchatton become aware of it, they show themselves too weak to face it. They refuse to face a world so grim and great as this world really is. They take refuge in stories of hauntings and personal madness—in the hope of some sort of exorcism, something they think will be a cure. . . . There is no such cure. There is no such way now of dressing up these facts and putting them aside.

"So, Sir, they have to be faced," he roared. "They have to be faced." He seemed to be addressing himself not simply to me but to some large public meeting. His vast gestures ignored me. "The time when men could be put in blinkers to save them from seeing too much is past.

Past for ever! There can be no more religions of reassurance. No churches of 'There—there!' *That* sort of thing is at an end."

"And then?" said I very quietly. Because the louder he shouted, the more coldly resistant I became.

He sat down and gripped my arm again. He became persuasively confidential. From bawling, his voice sank to a deep heavy undertone. "Madness, Sir, from the mental side, is poor Nature's answer to overwhelming fact. It is flight. And today all over the world, *intellectual men are going mad!* They are dithering, because they realize that the fight against this cave man who is over us, who is in us, who is indeed *us*, is going against these imaginary selves. The world is no longer safe for anything. It was sheer delusion that we had Him under. Him! The pursuing brute who never desists."

By a movement that I hoped seemed inadvertent, I freed my arm from his clutch. I had an absurd feeling that I was like that wedding guest who was gripped by the ancient mariner. "But then," I said, putting my hands in my pockets and leaning back so as to be out of reach of any fresh attempt to grab me, "what do you think you are doing with Finchatton? What do you think has to be done?"

Dr. Norbert waved his arms about and then stood up. "I tell you, Sir," he said, shouting down at me as though I was a score of yards off, "in the end he has to do what we all have to do. Face the facts! Face the facts, Sir! Go through with it. Survive if you can and perish if you can't. Do as I have done and shape your mind to a new scale. Only giants can save the world from complete relapse—and so we—we who care for civilization—have to become giants. We have to bind a harder, stronger civilization like steel about the world. We have to make such a mental effort as the stars have never witnessed yet. Arise, O Mind of Man!" (He called me that!) "Or be for ever defeated."

I wanted to say I preferred to be defeated without making any fuss about it, but he gave me no chance to say that.

For now indeed he was fairly raving. There was even a touch of froth on his lips. He paced up and down and talked on and on, in a fine frenzy.

I suppose from first to last throughout the ages

decent people of my sort have had to listen to this kind of thing, but it seemed to me beyond all reason that I should have to listen to it on the terrace of the Source Hotel at Perona above Les Noupets on a lovely morning in this year of grace nineteen hundred and thirty-six. He was striding up and down now like a Hebrew prophet. It may look all right as a part of history, this sort of rhetoric, this epoch-making and all that, but in real life it is hoarse and outrageous. It's damned bad manners—to be plain about it. I ceased to mark or remember half the things he said.

There was no answering it. One could as soon swim up the falls of Niagara.

He made it more and more plain that he was exhorting me. Me personally. I never had such a ballyragging. He was warning me to brace my mind to escape the Wrath to Come. He called it that—"Wrath to Come." He made me think of Peter the Hermit raging through the quiet cities of eleventh-century Christendom and starting all that trouble about the Crusades. He made me think of Savonarola and John Knox and all the disturbing people who have rushed shouting across history—leaving it very much as they found it—

telling people to give up their lives, go to their tents, O Israel, take up arms, storm the Tuileries, smash the Winter Palace, and a score of such outrageous things. At little old Les Noupets, mind you.

He reeled off a list of atrocities, murders, and horrors all over the world. I suppose there *is* a rather unusual amount of massacre and torture going on nowadays. I suppose the outlook *is* pretty black. I suppose there may be frightful wars, airraids, and pogroms ahead of us. But what am *I* to do about it? What was the good of bow-wowwowing at me? The intensity of his manner could not hide the fact that he had no certitude even in his own mind, that at best he was struggling with only the blank shadows of ideas. Whenever I tried to get in an inquiring word, he would raise his voice and boom over me. "I tell you," he would roar up.

But that was just what he didn't do—and apparently couldn't do.

"In a little while," he said, "there will be no ease, no security, no comfort any more." (Thank Heaven! he did not say I was "living on the brink of a volcano.") "There will be no choice before a human being but to be either a driven animal or a stern devotee to that true civilization, that disciplined civilization, that has never yet been achieved. Victim or Vigilante. And that, my friend, means you! I say it to *you*! *You!*" And he pointed a lean forefinger.

As there was no one else present—for the waiter had gone inside—there was no reason whatever for that "you" and that pointing finger. Just want of proportion. . . .

Yet— It is a most unpleasant thing to admit, but these two men *have* in a sort of way hypnotized me after all, and put something of this anxiety and something of this haunting of theirs upon me. I try and get them in a proper perspective by writing down this story, but the mere writing of it makes me realize how much I can't detach myself. I can no more get rid of it by telling it to you than Finchatton could get rid of it by telling it to me. I did not know that one could be hypnotized in this fashion, by people just sitting about or talking to you. I thought you had to sit still and give yourself up to hypnotism or else there was nothing doing. But now I find I don't sleep as well as I used to do, I catch myself anxious

about world affairs, I read evil things between
the lines in the newspapers, and usually very faintly
but sometimes quite plainly I see, behind the trans-
parent front of things, that cave-man face. . . .
How was it Finchatton put it—"continually rising and yet always towering there"? And I have
to admit I am not so even-tempered as I was in
conversation. The other day I even contradicted
my aunt with some asperity, to our mutual as-
tonishment. And I snapped at a waiter. . . .

I did not realize the seriousness of this business
until I had this scene with Norbert. That was
what made me so restive, and after I broke away
from him I took care to see no more of him or
Finchatton. Yet all the same the mischief had been
started in me and it grows. In those two brief
mornings, I got myself infected, fool that I was
to listen to them! And now the infection is working in me.

I resent the whole business. What is the good
of putting this horror of Cainsmarsh upon a man
and not telling him exactly what to do about it?
I *do* realize that our present world is going to
pieces. I quite see that we are still under the sway
of the cave man and that he is staging a tremen-

dous come-back. I am surprised I didn't see all that before. Already I have dreams about that giant skull, quite unpleasant dreams. But what is the good of talking about them? If I told my aunt any of this, she would say I was off my head. What can a fellow like me do about it all?

Study it up—enlarge my mind to a new scale? Become "giant-minded"? *What* a phrase! Build up a new civilization of steel and power in the place of the one that is collapsing? . . . Me? . . . Look at my bringing up! Is it *in* me?

It is too much to expect of our sort of people.

I'm ready to fall in with anything that seems promising. I'm all for peace, order, social justice, service, and all that. But if I'm to *think*! If I'm to find out what to do with myself!

That's too much.

I made my break-away from Norbert's flooding eloquence that morning with some considerable difficulty. I stood up. "I must be going," I said. "I have to play croquet with my aunt at half-past twelve."

"But what does croquet matter," he cried in that intolerable voice of his, "if your world is falling in ruins about you?"

He made a move almost as though he would impede my retreat. He just wanted to go on being apocalyptic. But I had had enough of this apocalyptic stuff.

I looked him in the face, firmly but politely. I said: "I don't care. The world *may* be going to pieces. The Stone Age may be returning. This may, as you say, be the sunset of civilization. I'm sorry, but I can't help it this morning. I have other engagements. All the same—laws of the Medes and Persians—I am going to play croquet with my aunt at half-past twelve today."